AF439306

DANGO DURANGO
The Bounty Hunter Series
Book 3
Escapes to Hangmans Creek

DAVID L. McADAMS

For information contact: info@Palehorsepublications.com
Cover Art by Michael Thomas
Cover Design by Pale Horse Publications
Published by Pale Horse Publications
September 2022
10987654321

Prologue

Mentions to characters and events from other books in the Dango Durango Bounty Hunter series do come up from time to time in this book. However, it's not necessary to read other books in the series first to have full enjoyment of this book. It is possible to read them in any order and not feel lost or like you are missing something, other than the normal twists and turns on the trail the author takes you on in this journey with Dango. Enjoy.

Chapter One

Clankie Claster ran from the woods almost as fast as his legs would carry him. His evil eyes were pale blue, traits he had inherited from his white ma. His brownish, dark skin was a combination of things, the fact that he spent most of his days outdoors and Mexican blood somewhere in his family line. The tan skin was coarse, almost as rough as his mannerisms.

Aiming his lever action, Henry sixteen-shooter, he fired and missed. But it was enough to cause the horse to rare back and throw its rider. Clankie jumped at the opportunity as the rider hit hard on the solid ground and had the wind knocked out of him.

"You know I'll have to kill you!"

The rider didn't respond, still dazed from the shock of the horse throwing him and the precarious landing.

Clankie stared at him a moment, just long enough for the rider to get enough wherewithal to lift his head and turn to look at him. When he did, the star on his vest became visible.

Clankie wasn't moved by the star. "You know I'll have to kill you!" He spit a dark spurt of snuff on the dusty ground, raised his sixteen-shooter, BAM! One shot was all it took. The rider didn't just slump over to death; he fell over suddenly, dead weight fast. His head hit the ground almost as quickly as the bullet had reached his chest when it left Clankie's rifle.

Clankie's next thought was to catch that horse. He reckoned the rider with the star pinned to his vest was part of the posse out looking for him. Feeling the need to hurry, he aimed his gaze to spot the spooked horse, his first thought being, *Well I know that horse*.

He whistled, not concerned the posse might hear and come running. If they hadn't heard the gunfire, he'd be okay. He didn't always think sensibly. If asked, there weren't many others who could outsmart him. For example, he had recently left several men hanging from several nooses, and here he was on the run, free instead of dead.

I know that horse! Recognition came as he tried coaxing the majestic Barb horse over to him. Clankie's previous gang leader had owned the brute of a horse. It had been stolen from a former slave master who was hung in the barn by his slave.

Before that, the horse came from Indians who had gotten it from Spanish Conquistadors who explored this part of the world. Ghengis, a Barb horse had been used when the Moors invaded Spain. The main reason the Barbs were used was because they were barbaric.

Clankie didn't even wonder why Ghengis had been startled by the bullet fire from his Henry. If he'd thought it out, he'd realized Ghengis was still not his normal sturdy self since his owner, Clankie's former gang leader had been hanged.

It didn't take long before Ghengis recognized Clankie and came over to him. He seemed to need somebody to trust. Clankie patted the side of his head and rubbed the front of his nose,

"That's a good boy Ghengis. Come on boy. I need a horse, and you definitely need somebody that'll keep you busy breaking laws instead of chasing lawbreakers."

He hopped on Ghengis without any objections from the Barb dun horse. Away they went, next stop who knows where. They picked up speed and sprinted in the opposite direction than where the rider with the star had come.

Just before this…

Clankie Claster had hidden in the woods near Lone Creek, Texas for almost half a week before he felt safe to come out from his hiding spot. This close to town, the pines grew thick. The farther out of town you went, pine trees became sparse and cactus and Joshua Trees took over.

Didn't think I'd make it out of it that time. His irrational mind was having a rare episode of making sense. Clankie was as mean as they come; he'd just escaped hanging at the gallows through a series of events that just happened to fall his way.

As him and the rest of the gang that had been arrested were marched to their executions, about to swing by their necks, he fell off the horse just before it was slapped out from underneath him. One of the reserve posse members who'd been sworn in long enough to provide security for the hanging, got startled and cut the rope.

Clankie's thinking was usually muddled, but as he was sneaking out of the forest at Lone Creek, he remembered very clearly the happenings that allowed his escape. He was sitting on the horse the executioner had prepared for him to be sitting on. The other gang members were each sitting on horses prepared for them.

Each outlaw had a heavy, dusty, burlap, hooded cover slipped over his head. Clankie wasn't sure if this was to prevent them from seeing their own execution or if it was to protect the witnesses from seeing the condemned bandit's eyes bulge out, faces change colors, and drool pour from their mouths and noses as their necks broke and they were strangled while hanging at the end of the rope.

He'd never heard of it happening this way, but here it was. The outlaws sentenced to death sat on the horses just before swinging from the gallows. The execution plan was for the horses to be slapped so they would run out from under the desperadoes sitting on them. This would leave the guilty criminals hanging till dead as the onlookers watched.

However, the horse Clankie Claster was sitting on, for one reason or another, spooked and took off early before the executioner had planned. When the horse took off, the posse member who was a volunteer deputy also got startled.

He was sitting on his own horse, and by sheer reaction, without planning, he pulled his ten inch knife from its scabbard and reached over and sliced the rope Clankie was swinging from. He would never be able to fully give an explanation that made sense to anyone who asked. Just one of those spur of the moment things where he made the wrong impulsive call.

Clankie ran at that moment as hard as he could. The dusty cover over his head didn't keep him from running. The cut piece of rope that was still around his neck didn't stop him from running. He was thankful they didn't hang criminals in Lone Creek with iron shackles on their wrists. That would've made his escape a whole lot harder. *He ran.*

The sudden unexpectedness of the whole situation worked to his advantage. What that part time reserve deputy did just didn't make any sense at all. It made so little sense that nobody's brain in the whole area that day registered quickly enough to allow the hooded outlaw to be captured before he got away.

So Clankie ran. He ran fast, He bumped into trees, beat through bushes and briars. The whole time he was running, his mind was subconsciously counting at a fast, thumping pace *one, two, three, four, five, six, seven…*

It was always one through seven. *Always.* His mind whirled as he was running. Once he got that blasted hood from over his head, he could tell you every color, every single item, everything he encountered between the site of the hanging gallows and the woods of Lone Creek. The entire time he was running and mentally counting, his mind was noticing everything. *Everything.*

And now, here he sat, in the forest on the outskirts of town. He knew Lone Creek wasn't a good town to return to once he got up the nerve to leave his hiding place. He would run as far away from here as it took, even if he had to leave Texas. He'd do whatever it took to avoid capture. He just knew luck had shined on him, and he wasn't about to let this chance go to waste.

Sitting in the woods, unable to slow his mind, he was counting quickly. One through seven. *I'll find someplace where they've never heard the name Clankie Claster or the name of the gang I've ridden with.* He looked at the revolver on his hip. *If not, I'll kill everybody it takes to make sure I don't ever have another rope around my neck.*

Chapter Two

Clankie had finally left the safety of the wooded area just outside Lone Creek. He had been certain they would capture him when he heard the hound dogs baying. Those red bloodhounds have keen senses, and their moan is so deep and loud, it seemed they had to be in the same patch of woods with him at least a time or two.

After more than a full night of not hearing them dogs wailing, he had become determined to make a run for it. As soon as he had raced from the woods, he heard the horse hooves hitting the ground, looked that direction and saw the lawman and shot him in the chest. Right after that, he had whistled for the horse he'd recognized.

Now, he sat atop Ghengis, sprinting at a good stride. They'd been at it several hours with no sign of a posse or anybody else following. Coming over a slight ridge, Clankie was captivated by the sight as soon as they topped the sloped hill.

"Would you look at that boy?"

Just ahead, what looked like several hundred heads of cattle were being herded toward the northwest. He immediately knew they were longhorns. It was a parade of livestock. Most were reddish tan and others were brown with white patches and spots. Some were dark brown. A few of them were solid black, and a few more were black with white, splotched markings.

These cattle have horns ranging from six to seven feet across. Their breed line first came to Texas through a series of events that included Christopher Columbus' travels and the colonizing of Spaniards near Texas ranges. They can adapt to extreme heat, high humidity, extreme cold, and drought. They are very docile, and the cows generally range from 950 to 1,200 pounds, while the bulls normally weigh in at 1,200 to 2,000 pounds. The longhorns have long legs, thick hooves, and round bodies. Typically, they grow to between four and five feet tall.

It looked like an organized stampede. Dango didn't even think to wonder why he hadn't noticed the dust the cattle were kicking into the air before he had come over the ridge. The herd reached a sandbar, heading toward a creek. He thought, *There looks like at least a thousand of 'em. Surely there can't be that many.*

They were moving at a decent speed, being force-marched. Several cowhands rode along the perimeter of the herd, screaming, "Yah!" as they drove the cattle in a particular direction. As the longhorns lumbered from the sandbar into the creek, Dango noticed it quickly came about belly deep to them before they had to give in to swimming.

Blowing dust covered the air approaching the sandbar, and the whole scene was barely visible to Clankie. He'd been on enough cattle drives and sand storms to be able to look through the dust and use his limited vision combined with his imagination to have a pretty good understanding of what he was witnessing.

Nosiness caused him to follow through the dust a little bit back from the herd of bovines. He didn't want the cowhands to suspect him of being there for rustling and stir up more problems for him just yet. He usually welcomed trouble, but right now he was ready to find a hot meal somewhere and rest his weary bones for a bit before hitting it hard again.

Once the last of the cattle cleared the wide, strong-tea colored creek on the other side, Clankie reckoned it was okay for him to cross. Ghengis walked into the water and tramped as far as he could before having to swim through the deepest part.

Once they sauntered up on the bank on the northwest side of the creek, Dango saw three nooses dropped from the limbs of three live oak trees. Then, he noticed a crudely fashioned board sign with the name of the place scrawled on it, *Hangmans Creek, Texas.*

Clankie made a quick, rash decision that this would be a good place to hide out for a while. After all, in his thinking, *who would expect a murderer to be crazy enough to stop at a place with a name like Hangmans Creek?*

Chapter Three

Dango tossed and turned for more than an hour before finally giving up on trying. Sitting up in bed, he stared into the darkness, feeling Savannah's warm body right next to him. His restlessness hadn't disturbed her sleep at all.

Savannah was a soul mate to Dango, no doubt about it. Daily, she would find ways to show her love, go out of her way to make sure he was at peace, kiss him just out of the blue, say *I love you* without him saying it first.

He knew she had worked hard all day and into the evening before they retired for the night. He wasn't even tempted to hold it against her for lying there sleeping hard while he had tried his best to go back to sleep and finally resorted to being awake in the middle of the night.

The bed he was lying in was very comfortable. The woman next to him was extremely alluring. After the wedding, they had spent time on a long honeymoon. It was time well spent, riding the enormous Creole Princess paddle wheel boat on the Mississippi. After leaving the Mississippi River, the newlyweds had spent the rest of their honeymoon leisurely taking their time while making the trip back to Colorado.

The bedroom they were in was as nice as any in the area.

It had the workmanship of Dango's hard laboring and the love he poured into building the home, knowing he was preparing it for Savannah and him to grow old together.

The poem he had written for her and read at their wedding was framed and hung on the bedroom wall. Besides the bedroom, the log home had a combined kitchen and eating area, a living space in the front of the house, and the outhouse out back.

The home sat on too many wooded acres for one couple. The mountainous area of their property remained covered with timber. Blue spruces and white aspen trees mixed well to colourfully paint the mountain sides. The home was situated near the foot of the mountains in a meadow that was perfect for cattle grazing. It was hard to tell where the yard area ended and the pastures began, since stunning deep green grass grew abundantly.

All this perfection and Dango could not sleep. His mind was just where Savannah knew it would be when she said *I do*. She realized his very soul, his life's work, his calling was on the trail chasing the bounty. She didn't feel cheated or robbed, just the opposite actually. Dango loved her, and she didn't have any doubts.

Realizing it was in his blood, something he couldn't get away from, she would never try to gain leverage to keep him home when it was time to go. That said; she would love for him to always be there to touch, to hold, to look into his dark, piercing eyes.

She knew, however, if he was forced to stay when it was time for pursuit, those piercing eyes would grow dull, dim, and distant.

Dango turned back over on one side, determined to fall back to sleep. He would lay there several more hours without sleep coming. Come daylight, Savannah would be awake enough for him to let her know it was time to go again. He had a feeling she already knew it.

He had word that Clankie Claster had escaped from the hanging gallows down in Texas. He couldn't sleep knowing that killer was on the loose, and innocent people were in harm's way. Thinking of the violent incident that happened at Ernie's Trading Square in Lone Creek, Texas, he knew he wouldn't rest until Clankie was back in prison and had a renewed date with a hanging lasso.

Chapter Four

After Savannah woke up, Dango had talked to her about his plans. That had been early this morning, and he'd been riding most of the day. With a little more than an hour before sundown, he was approaching his old friend's ranch. There had been two weddings and two honeymoons since the last time he'd been here.

Dango had married Savannah and spent time cruising on the mighty Mississippi, then took a long, scenic route through Arkansas, Oklahoma, Texas, New Mexico, and back into Colorado.

Tumbleweed, who used to ride bounties with Dango, had married Pricilla, the young Mexican woman he'd taken into his home, and took her on the best honeymoon she could dream of, back to the Yucatan Peninsula. They visited the pyramids and ruins, but the best part of the trip, besides being together, was seeing her family who lived in the Yucatan.

Dango was immediately allowed entry by the gunhand at the entrance gate of the Circle W Ranch. Twilight went on a direct course from the entry gate to Tumbleweed's home, which was situated on a northwest angle from the ranch's operation building.

Dango's friend Tumbleweed, who he called Weed, had built the magnificent ranch from the ground up several years ago.

He had come here with dreams of building a ranch, marrying, and raising children. So far, two of those dreams had come to fruition. They were still waiting for children to come along.

As Dango and Twilight rode up to the main house, two massive, reddish-tan Bull Mastiffs rushed over, barking in their deep, menacing tones. As soon as they recognized who it was, the barks turned from malice to friendliness.

Weed heard all the commotion and came to the door with his shotgun in tow. As soon as he peeked out the door, he noticed the change in barking sounds Furious and Ferocious were making. Then he saw Dango and Twilight.

Dango hopped from the saddle and headed to the front door of the homestead at a determined pace. He hadn't seen his old friend in a while and was hankering to catch up. They had a lot of history together and he felt like they still had a ton of memories to make together.

Weed grinned from ear to ear as he waited for his confrère to reach him at the front door to his home. He was actually more than one who had simply shared professional, working employment with him. He was one of his truest and dearest lifelong friends. "Dango. Come on in friend. How's married life treating you?"

Dango couldn't help from beaming like a starved man being served fried venison over a bed of steamed rice with gravy. "Mighty fine Weed. How about you?"

"Couldn't be any better. I never dreamed it to be as good as it is. And you know I dreamed of the right girl for a long time."

They both laughed at this, realizing just how true it was. Weed had come to the dreariness of thinking he'd never meet the right female, one who would see through his hard shell and discover that there was a decent, sweet intuitiveness inside him.

After being invited in, Dango spent the better part of a couple hours catching up with Weed and Pricilla on each of the couple's honeymoon trips and then finding their way into the eating area where Turnip had steamy vittles ready to be devoured.

Once the catching up and eating was accomplished, he finally got around to the main reason for the visit. "Heading down Texas way, thought you might want to go out there with me after this bounty."

Weed looked down from his six-four frame, seeming even taller with his erect posture, felt Stetson, and leather boots. He never had been able to tell Dango no.

Actually, every time he'd ever been asked to go somewhere like this with him, it seemed like he'd been offered to go on an adventure. Kind of like when pa took him fishing when he was a young boy.

The thought *no* had never come into play. Never crossed his mind. It was always an instinctive *yes*.

"Heck yeah, I'll go." Looking instantly at Pricilla, he could see in her eyes her acceptance. However, in that acceptance, he knew there also existed a twinge of pain. There was always a presence of missing each other when not together.

"There's a bounty supposed to be out there who I apprehended once already. Apparently, they let him get away after the noose was already around his neck. This one as hardened as they come Weed. If he's not stopped, he's sure to kill more. That's who he is, and I'm convinced there ain't no amount of trying to help him see the error of his ways that will do him any good."

Dango's face had a grim, determining expression as he continued, "I personally know of several cold-hearted, callous crimes he's committed. Don't matter to him if it's a man, woman, child, young or elderly that he's gunning for; he's that nasty of a varmint. "

"He sounds troubled and ruthless. I pray he can be stopped before causing any more killing. How in the world did he get out of the rope once it was around his grimy neck? Has to be a story behind that."

"You got that right. I think we can be the ones who find him and stop him from doing any more bloodbaths. Let me tell you all about how he got away from the executioner's noose."

Weed, Pricilla, and Turnip all listened attentively as Dango filled them in on the escape of Clankie Claster from the hangman's rope. They'd get a good night's rest and head out the next morning.

The way Pricilla kissed Weed early the next morning as they said their goodbyes reminded Dango again of how much he missed Savannah. He knew Clankie had to be rearrested. Once that was done, the reuniting back at home in Colorado with her would be more satisfying than the longing now was empty.

As Dango and Weed rode along on their horses, heading to catch a train to Texas, they ruminated over times spent together chasing bounties. Neither of them had a true count of how many they'd caught. Didn't even know if the ratio was higher for those captured dead or alive.

"How about the time ol' Jack Bender tried to waylay you by surprise?"

"Ha ha." Dango chuckled, "That ambush might've worked too, if he would've realized there were two of us walking through there that night."

"Yeah, I wish I could've seen the look of shock on his face when he jumped for you and I conked him upside the back of the head."

"From the position where I was standing, I did see his flabbergasted look. I think it was frozen on his face when he fell."

At this, they both laughed heartily, two bounty hunters and their stories.

"Ha ha ha ha ha ha . And how about the time…"

Chapter Five

Farmers Crossing used to be a bustling town on the way to somewhere. It had been a stop in the road for travelers to restock and go on their way to wherever they were heading. A farming family had seen the prospect of establishing a settlement here and began to scratch out a living selling produce, fruit, and supplies. Before long, families started arriving, and the small stop in the dusty trail turned into a blossoming town.

It wasn't long though until ranchers moved in up the road and started trying to build up their own encampment. They brought men with guns and girls who knew how to dance. It almost seemed like overnight that they had a saloon up and running. The encampment grew into a town, and that first building, the saloon, was crowded every night with rambunctious happenings.

Businessmen noticed the money funneling through the saloon, and without even forming a committee or taking a vote, other buildings were thrown up in this new town.

The businessmen were blinded by the potential for money and didn't give one speck of thought to the notion of men with guns roaming the streets. The guns were filled with bullets, and the gunmen spent most of their time filled with alcohol from the Watering Hole. A deadly combination.

The prosperity of this new place led to the demise of Farmers Crossing just down the road a piece. The farmers eventually struck out on their own, finding a spot farther from where they'd tried to build up a stop in the road.

They would scrape out their own living for a while, trying to build up their own town, until the ranchers and men with guns would eventually drive them away entirely. Farmers Crossing became a ghost town. Just up the road a little over an hour's ride by horse, the town founded by the ranchers became known as Hangmans Creek.

Unbeknownst to others, two old codgers had moved into the forsaken Farmers Crossing. Hurley Jenkins and Wilford Waterman were the founding members of the Wild Bumpkins Gang. They had come up with the name of the gang themselves and prided themselves in that.

The actual name itself was one-third self-fulfilling prophecy. They're not as wild as they believe themselves to be. They're not a gang in the sense that they think they are. However, they are as bumpkin as they come.

Each of the men would fit in just fine in the woods with a moonshine operation, on the porch wearing overalls whittling away the hours in a rocking chair, or chasing away good guys in their dreams while they took their loot from them. Wilford likes being called Waco, and that's what he refers to himself as. Hurley likes being called Hurley. An ornery pair, as unsophisticated as they come.

People passing by may think they actually see ghosts in this old deserted town, however, it's just glances of ol' Wilford and Hurley moving about while trying to stay hidden. The two curmudgeons made a makeshift sign that used the word WILD as an acrostic. They figure the sign will either bring them notoriety or passersby will just think it belonged to somebody who lived here when the town was booming.

The sign reads: *WILD*

What I Love to Do

Every so often Hurley and Wilford will work themselves up in a lather of commotion over the sign, using it as a prod to get their blood pumping for violence. Their main goal, as they've agreed to, is to spread violence as a way of gaining a fortune. To date, they've managed to hurt a few people, including themselves on occasion, but have not gotten many treasures to speak of out of their gang's undertakings.

Hurley sounded like an evangelistic preacher as he used that old sign religiously, "What I love to do Waco is go into town and see just how much fear I can preevoke in the people!"

Wilford's response was just like Hurley's; it didn't follow any grammar rules of higher circles, but they meshed very well together, two old bumpkin cranks with similar values or lack of values, comparable morals or absence of morals, and the same way of thinking.

"You're dadgum right Hurley! We can preevoke 'em to fear and stur up the whole town for shore."

Wilford, the self-acclaimed Waco, went on with his raving, using the saying they'd come up with on the sign, "What I love to do is hurt 'em as bad as they kin be hurt. Then they'll turn loose of thare money. Won't have no choice. They'll be in so much hurtin' and be so a skeered, they'll be begging us to take thare money."

Even though the sign that Hurley and Wilford had scribbled out had the word love on it, neither of them had an ounce of love in him. They were uncompassionate, grizzled characters. Although they didn't reach the heights or lows of missing compassion as some of the infamous gunfighters in the wild west, they were missing any sparkle of love in their hearts.

They were filled with carnal hankerings in themselves that drove them to do everything they did. Every single thing. Not an action was made without it being one that met a fleshly longing within. The cravings of their pleasure-seeking appetites had to be fed. Like wild cattle being herded, they were driven by inner desires. Turned out to be more of a mad dash most of the time.

Neither of them had shot at anybody, attempted to hold-up somebody, or threatened another person except it fulfilled their own need for respect, something neither of them would get any other way. They didn't even respect one another, argued more than anything else. But that arguing itself seemed somehow to satisfy a need they each had.

The two old men didn't have any idea they were about to cross paths with one of the nastiest legends of their time, Clankie Claster. If they had a clue this was about to take place, it would be a sleepless night for them.

Chapter Six

Clankie figured he'd scout around town and get the gist of the place. Especially being curious about how he could stir up some trouble and bring a lot of greenbacks his way at the same time, he would be sure and notice anything of interest.

In all his snooping, he definitely wanted to find out why in blazes this place was called Hangmans Creek. Figuring it had something to do with the hanging nooses near the creek he'd crossed coming into town, he knew there had to be more to it than that.

Noticing the Watering Hole still had a few customers, he stopped in for a quick drink. He reckoned this would be more of a hasty visit to grab something wet and case the place. While standing at the bar with only a handful of patrons left milling around and all of them sloppy drunk, he just knew he was already onto something.

Surely the days take was still in the cash box or the safe. The clientele was inebriated and the staff was tired. He poured the rest of his drink down in one swish and turned to leave, determined to come back prepared and take the place for all it was worth.

Riding through the dead town, the air was still, the night dark. A waning crescent moon hung low in the sky. Something caught the corner of Clankie's eye.

Peering that direction it looked in the night's dimness like somebody hanging in the air. As he drew closer, he noticed it was two people hanging. Going nearer, he noticed they were not hanging, they were holding on. He was finally close enough to take it in, two ignoramuses were holding onto a rope that was dangling from a sturdy limb.

Dango got close enough to hear the two men and what he heard was as senseless as what he was witnessing. One of the men had curly gray hair covering his entire head. The other was almost bald with a little bit of white hair on either side of his head.

Balding said, "Wilford, you've got to bounce more. Try harder."

Curly gray replied, "That's Waco to you. You just tend to your bouncing, and I'll tend to mine."

"Well if you was tending to yours right, I wouldn't have to say nuthing about it."

Before balding or curly gray could carry on with anymore of the quarrelling, one of them spotted the mean looking, tan cowboy on the nasty looking steed. Then the other one saw him too. Dropping from the rope like they'd been caught red handed, they stood there not knowing what to say or how to react.

Clankie started the conversation with the two, "Well I admit it, y'all have me confused."

Neither man answered. Hurley and Wilford both just stood there underneath the hanging rope, hoping the stranger would just ride on if they didn't respond.

"What are you two ol' fools doing out here?"

Clankie looked closer at the situation while waiting for an answer. The rope had been thrown over a solid tree limb that extended out over the local bank. Apparently the two had thrown the rope over the limb and fastened a hook at one end of it.

They had attached the hook to the bottom of the tin roof of the bank and were trying their hardest to jerk the rope at the other end in hopes the tin roof would be pulled off the bank.

That's why they were having a squabble about who was and who wasn't bouncing hard enough. It all made sense now. Well, it didn't really make sense, but it was clear now what the two had been trying to do when he rode up.

"I'll tell you what, you ain't never gonna get this here bank robbed the way you're going at it. How about let's get all this equipment picked up and go somewhere a little more private? Then, I'll show you gents how we can get everything they've got in this here bank."

Hurley and Wilford didn't say a word. They just both went to picking up their stuff. As they hopped on their horses and headed out, neither of them had said anything yet. Clankie rode along on Ghengis, following close behind, knowing he'd found some old-timers he could trust.

Chapter Seven

"This here's Hurley and I'm Waco." The two had finally started talking to Clankie.

"Waco? I thought I heard him calling you Wilbur or something."

"Wilbur? No. He was calling me Wilford. That's my name."

"Wilford? I thought you just now said you was Waco."

"That's the name I go by, Waco. My given name is Wilford, but I like to go by Waco."

"Oh. Ok. I guess I'll call you Waco then. How about you Hurley? Is it Hurley, or should I call you something else too?"

"No, it's just Hurley. Hurley will do just fine."

Both men had naturally shaky voices. It was hard to tell if they were nervous, scared, or just unstable. The quiver in their voices made one wonder if their hands would tremble when handling a gun.

Hurley continued proudly in his unsteady voice, "We're the Wild Bumpkins Gang."

"The Wild Bumpkins Gang? Ain't that something? Right here in the flesh. Never heard of you."

"Well maybe you haven't, but you will. You mark my word."

"Well I have now. I'm standing here talking to you ain't I?"

"Oh yeah, well I suppose you are."

"So tell me, what's the Wild Bumpkins Gang?"

Wilford took over, "We came up with that ourselves. Get folks to thinking we ain't got no sense. Then we can outfox 'em without 'em knowing it."

Clankie thought back to when he first met the two men and thought better of what *Waco* had just told him. Didn't seem too smart trying to hook a roof off a bank.

"Talking about outfoxing somebody, let me tell you about how I ended up here."

Both members of the Wild Bumpkins Gang were wide-eyed and ready to hear what Clankie was about to tell them.

"It all began with a bounty hunter named Dango Durango chasing me and the rest of my gang. There was injuns and all kinds of wild things going on. You call yourselves the Wild Bumpkins Gang. Let me tell you about wild."

They didn't say a peep. Clankie wondered if they were even breathing. "They had the rope around my neck, had me sitting on a horse. Next thing I knew the horse took off running out from under me, and I fell with a jolt, hard and sudden like. I was hanging by the neck wondering how long it would be before I was dead. Then all of a sudden, I fell and hit the hard ground hard."

"You hit the hard ground hard?"

"I hit the *hard* ground *hard.*"

Both men gasped as Clankie continued, "I didn't know if I was still alive or if this was how death felt. I was scared. It was dark. I was hurting from hitting the ground with that dang blasted hood over my head."

"What do ya mean? What kind of hood?"

"They put some sort of heavy cover over my head before they hung me. Felt like burlap or canvas, something heavy. It smelled like it had been used to hang somebody else before. Like a dead man's head had already been inside it. It was dark. I couldn't hardly breathe. When I dropped and was hanging by that rope, I couldn't breathe at all. Then when I fell and hit the ground, it knocked what little bit of air I had in my lungs out."

"How'd the rope break?"

"Not really sure. Maybe it was rotten. Shor' glad it did though."

Wilford and Hurley hung onto every word.

"I started running. Even before I thought to get that danged hood off of my head, I ran as fast as I could. I ended up in some strange woods I'd never been in before.

Redbone hounds kept coming into the woods and baying, howling, and barking. I'm not sure how many days and nights I was in them woods before luck shined on me and I shot a lawman and took the horse he stole off ol' Zeke Scott."

Wilford Waco Waterman and Hurley Jenkins said at the same exact time, "*Zeke Zulu Scott?*"

"The one and the same."

"You rode with the Zulu Outlaws?"

Clankie couldn't help but let his pride show as he failed to suppress a smile, "Shore nuff."

Hurley retorted, "Then that horse you been riding must be the notorious Ghengis."

"You boys ain't so dumb after all."

Chapter Eight

The nearest rail depot was about a day's ride from Lone Creek by horse. Dango and Weed had ridden all day after the long train trip. Then they'd fed, watered, and bedded Twilight, Brown and White, and Hay Bale in the local livery stable before bedding themselves in a couple of rooms for rent over at the Triple Down.

Here you could find lodging, eating, and drinking. When asked about the name, it was told that you could wash it down, eat it down, or bed down all in one location. The rooms were upstairs, and the eating space and saloon area were both downstairs.

Weed's hefty, young bronco had been tamed at an earlier age. He was a rough bronc, but had been trained through use to give Weed a gentle enough ride. Whether strolling at an easy pace or running at full gallop, his calmness for riding was felt in the saddle.

However, being the bronc that he was, his ways were usually rough and wild. He obeyed Weed unintuitively, as by nature he was inclined to do his own thing in his own ways. And those ways were typically brash and harsh. However, Weed had been firm enough when needed and forgiving enough as necessary to get ol' Hay Bale trained to be a horse that he could trust while keeping the strong ways he'd been born with.

It had been easy enough to give the young bronco a name. His pale yellow color and grassy mane led Weed to begin calling him Hay Bale from when they first met.

Brown and White had been working in bounty hunting with Dango for several years. His general duties consisted of transporting bad guys. His strong backbone helped him carry out his responsibilities with no regrets. He'd carried many outlaws strung across his back, and he'd been working with Dango and Twilight long enough to do what he was supposed to without much bossing from them.

Both men were early risers and came downstairs before daybreak to grab some strong coffee and early morning grub.

Sitting inside the Triple Down at a square, wooden table, Dango gestured at the inside of the place with his right hand that was holding a four tine, flatiron fork. "Weed, you ever seen a saloon with a layout quite like this?"

"Don't remember it if I have. This place is ginormous. Just the drinking area itself takes up more space than I've usually seen in saloons."

"And to have a full-fledged area dedicated just for dining. No wonder this is the only eating place in town. Ain't no need for any other."

"Last time I was here, the Stone family had a place you could eat at three times a day. Sounds like they moved back home down by the border. That's a shame too; they had some mighty fine eating at their restaurant."

"I doubt it was any better than this Dango." Weed continued shoveling in food while he was talking.

"Well, one thing, when their place was open, there wasn't any eating area in here."

"Well, what in the world did they do with this space back then? You told me the Stone family café was the only place to eat in town before."

"Don't really know. Maybe they added on here when the Stones moved back home."

Dango and Weed were sitting in an area of the Triple Down that was sectioned off for eating. There had to be at least a dozen tables with four chairs each. No partitions of any sort were in place, but customers could certainly tell this was the place in the saloon where food was served.

As soon as you walk in the batwing doors at the front of the place, you step right into the dancing area. Patrons looking to get a drink when they come in have to make their way through the dancing crowd. This early however, there are only a couple men in the place besides Dango, Weed, and the employees.

The owner of The Triple Down is rarely seen in these parts. He spends most of his time fishing the many rivers in this area of Texas and leaves Lincoln Nady to manage the place. He stops by once a month or two and takes his earnings, checking the books to make sure Lincoln and the other staff are being taken care of monetarily. He sees to it there's enough in the bank to keep the place running, and off to the river he goes.

The piano sits to the right of the dance floor, and going straight ahead from the entrance, across the dancing area is the bar where Lincoln Nady tends to serving drinks. His varied tasks include pouring drinks, overseeing the cook and both waitresses, tending to problems that arise in the place, especially when people get as full of alcohol as the place gets full of people.

"Any idea of where to start Dango?"

"Well, I'd say after we finish our hotcakes and links we go over and see Sheriff Lee. He's a fine man. You'll like him."

Weed chewed on his sausage and stuffed a fork full of pancakes dripping with huckleberry syrup into his mouth.

Dango took a long swig of his black coffee and continued, "Last time I was here, there was a big poker game going on."

Weed answered while chewing, "Oh yeah?"

"Yeah. Had Jackson P. Strider, Strychnine Jim, Big Bob Flowers, Lacy Laci, and Hoot-Owl Chappy all right here at the same time in a tournament."

Weed drained the rest of his hot cup and answered, "Man, I would've liked to have seen that."

"It was a good time. However, the competition was interrupted and they ended up finishing it someplace else." Dango laughed lightly as he recollected, "And I just happened upon them when they were finishing it."

"Just talking about it, you look like you really enjoyed that."

"Yeah I did. A riverboat on the Mississippi, poker masters, and the biggest week of my life. Those were great times."

In the dining area of a saloon in southeast Texas around sunrise, Dango suddenly missed Savannah more than he had since he'd left to head to Texas. He emptied his coffee mug down his throat, "How about we go see the sheriff."

Chapter Nine

"Sunday school teacher or not! I couldn't just let somebody call me out like that!"

Clankie Claster had spent the morning telling Hurley and Wilford stories about his gunfights, bank jobs, stagecoach holdups, and other illustrious happenings. They hadn't gotten out of bed very early, but did manage to crawl out before noon.

Wilford and Hurley were all ears, listening to Clankie's accounts, seeing him as a hero. After all, he had ridden with the notorious Zeke Scott.

"That teacher in the First Street Righteous Church told me I was going to hell! Said I was wicked and needed saving. I showed that Sunday school teacher just who needed saving!"

Hurley was glued to the conversation, but he managed to get some words out, "What happened next?"

"It was all going at a running fast pace. The teacher was telling me how bad I was! Then, I'd stand up for myself and scream that it was nobody's business but mine! Then, all of a sudden everything went to very slow motion. I raised my gun from its holster, aimed, and pressed the trigger harder than I'd ever pressed it. Everything around me seemed to become curvy and wavy and slow." He said the word *slow* as slowly as he could, drawing it out as long as he could for effect.

Wilford was able to get some words out, "Then, what happened after that?"

"Everything was still in really slow motion. My finger held the trigger pushed firmly back as hard as I could squeeze it. The bullet seemed to fly sluggishly from the barrel of my gun. It was almost like I could see it. It flew gracefully through the air. And after what seemed like a complete minute from the time it left my gun, everything suddenly sped way up again, and the bulled hit her just under her left eye. She would never call anybody else mean or wicked or evil or hateful again! Never again!"

Wilford and Hurley laughed loudly and stiffly, both almost losing their breath as they hooted and snorted.

After a long spell of several minutes, Hurley was able to talk through his laughing, "Served her right. You're one of the nicest persons we've ever met."

Wilford showed signs of agreeing, even though it would be several minutes before he could compose himself through the boisterous chuckling to be able to say anything.

When the cackling was starting to die down, Clankie ordered, "Okay, okay, let's get it together. We gotta get our plans together. I cased the saloon in a town down the road apiece and discovered just how we can take it for everything it's got."

"You talking about over at Lone Creek? Triple Down? Or the Watering Hole back over at Hangmans Creek?" Wilford asked.

"It's at that place with the nooses hanging right by a creek. I can take you to it and show you where it's at."

Clankie continued giving the two old men information, "Anyways, I went in and looked around, found a way to score without much effort. If we go in late enough after most everybody is gone and before the money is taken away for the day's earnings, we can bring in a big haul."

His audience became gleeful at the thought of pulling off a big job. He could see the gears turning in their old heads. "Y'all just let me do the thinking and this will work out for all of us."

Wilford answered by saying, "After the job's done, we can bring the stash back here to the Wild Bumpkins Gang's hideout and split it up."

Clankie looked around the ghost town they were holed up in. He saw the WILD sign the two bumpkins had crudely made. He saw derelict coach wagons that were used sometime in the past. He noticed dilapidated houses families had lived in previously. There were empty fruit and vegetable stands half standing and partially fallen. Several lots where buildings had once stood were now vacant, strewn with litter, and blackened by ash from fires gunhands had started.

Clankie went on with his directions, "That's a good idea Waco. We'll do the job, get the money, and bring it back here to divvy it up."

Wilford's eyes lit up when Clankie called him Waco.

Clankie continued, "We'll divide the loot. I'll take half, and you two can split the other half."

Hurley and Wilford nodded agreeably like they'd just been handed a birthday present. In their eyes, that was two for them and only one for Clankie. The laughing started up again.

Chapter Ten

The sun seemed like it had come up fast this morning. It was an orange, burning blur. The only thing that kept the ride tolerable was the nice breeze that had decent gusts every so often.

"There's another one!" Weed shouted as he and Dango held on tightly to their hats.

When the blast of air settled, Dango answered, "Cotton on it Weed. That felt as good as a hot bath after a long ride on the trail."

Weed smiled, knowing just what he meant. "Almost as good as Turnip's chili and cornbread."

"I wouldn't go that far."

Both men laughed again while craving the mouth-watering, chili and cornbread.

"Heck, you can eat the cornbread all by itself, it's so delicious." Weed said this like he hadn't eaten in a month.

Dango agreed, "Turnip's cornbread is better than most folk's cake."

At that true remark, Weed had a proud smugness wash over him, knowing he had a gem of a cook working for him.

"And just think, when we…"

"Both you, throw them guns down, we've got you surrounded!"

The stranger showed up from nowhere, pulling up hard in front of Dango and Weed, making demands and threats.

As they were pulling their horses to a quick stop to study the situation, the dark haired stranger dressed like he'd spent a year on a cattle drive barked more orders, "Hurry up! There's ten men in them woods waiting to pounce on you if'n you give me any trouble."

"Hold on son, let's just talk this out."

"Ain't gonna be no talking! I want your firearms and anything you've got worth anything."

The man must've been in his late twenties, appeared to have a hardness about him that he'd grown into. He yelled to the woods for effect, "Just keep your guns on 'em! I've got this all under control! They try anything funny, y'all let 'em have it!"

Dango and Weed glanced at the tree line. Neither of them saw any movement or heard any rustling nearby.

Dango offered, "Your friends hiding in them trees must surely be disguised as trees or something. They're blending in so good, I can't see 'em at all."

Weed added, "Or hear 'em either for that matter."

"I don't know what y'all are trying to suggest. They're there all right.

And besides that, even if'n they waren't, I can handle this all by myself. You won't be the first men I've killed, you try anythang funny. I've tangled with five men at a time, and I shorely killed 'em all. Ever' last one of 'em all at one time."

Dango and Weed were letting the stranger ramble. When he got so lost in his recollecting, both men saw they had the drop on him and fired at the same time.

The next thing that happened was the loud mouthed mucky man stopped his reminiscing, screamed in mid-sentence, and fell like a rock from his horse, hitting the ground with a thud. The next thing that didn't happen was the showing up of ten men running from the woods with guns firing.

Dango offered into the air while jumping from Twilight and rushing to close the space between himself and the stranger on the ground, "I didn't think there were any men with you in them woods."

The man on the ground was in too much pain to reply. All he could do right now was wail loudly and hold both arms near his muscles as he lay there squirming in pain. Dango had hit one of his biceps when he fired. Weed's shot had hit the man in the other arm.

They managed to get him hogtied on Brown and White while listening to his cries for some relief from the burning gashes the bullets had torn into his flesh.

Having done all they could do for him, they wondered two things, first *why did this goof try to tangle with two armed men all by himself,* and second, *why did Lone Creek have a stretch of road that seemed to be in the middle of nowhere between the Triple Down and the sheriff's office.*

"You know Dango, it's funny how some of these small towns do things."

"Yeah. Last time I was out this way, I never gave any thought to it. Seems like a nice ride through here, but I can see where bandits might think this a good ambush point."

"Well, at least the convicts at the jail are a ways from the rest of the population."

When Weed said that, he was thinking about the likes of the stranger they had secured on ol' Brown and White. He would hope every offender Sheriff Lee locked up would rehabilitate and assimilate back into society. Somehow, he'd have to really stretch his hope to think that about this hardened young man though.

Dango and Weed arrived at the jail with their newest apprehended lawbreaker. The jail that doubled as a courthouse was sitting in the middle of nowhere. There was a boardwalk in front and a place for hanging out back. Farther back, behind the hanging tree was an old cemetery with crude, grayish white headstones scattered about.

Just as Dango and Weed walked in, carrying the young man with a bullet hole in each arm, Sheriff Lee greeted them like this was a normal scene in his jail.

"Hello men. Whatcha got there?"

Weed noticed right away some things Dango already knew. The sheriff had a thick Texan accent. He was a colored man, about five feet ten inches. His stocky build was suitable for the barrel chest and large gut he carried. His sheriff star was pinned to a vest he wore over his long sleeve wool shirt.

"This young man tried to hold us up on the way over here sheriff."

Dango and Sheriff CW Lee shook hands like they were old friends. "This here is my good friend Tumbleweed."

"You gotta knack for bringing in hooligans who tried to bushwhack you Dango."

Dango knew Sheriff Lee said this from thinking back to another time the bounty hunter came through Lone Creek. He didn't answer, just smiled momentarily.

Weed and the sheriff shook hands with one another. "You can call me Weed sheriff. Nice to meet you."

As the sheriff and Weed were acknowledging one another, the young man woke from his pain induced slumber and started yelling in agony again, "Ohhhhhhh! Ohhhhhhh! Somebody help me!"

"This burning pain in my arms is too much!"

There was a drawback from being out here a ways from the center of town; doc's office was a decent ride away.

Sheriff Lee moved toward the hurting felon, "You men know who y'all have here?"

"Just some youngster who tried to trap us and rob us."

"This here's Jimmy Monrestic. I'm shor' surprised you ain't heard of him. He's held up and killed folks all over Texas."

"This young man?"

"Yes siree. Ol' Jimmy's been a pain from the border down south to the panhandle up north. He's evaded capture for more'n a year now. That sly little fox."

"Well, he ain't running no more."

The man was still bellowing while the men talked over who they had caught.

"I better lock him up and ride over to get Doc Gillon."

"Okay sheriff. If it's alright, we'll just wait here for you. Got some bounty business to discuss when you get back. Come all the way from Colorado looking for another fugitive."

That sparked a thought in the sheriff's brain, "Oh, that reminds me, y'all have a nice reward coming for bringing in Jimmy Monrestic. We'll square that up when I get back and go over your new order of business."

Sheriff Lee locked the bawling wrongdoer in one of the cells at the back of the jail. Dango and Weed could still hear his squalling as they waited up front near the sheriff's desk.

"I should be back in about an hour."

Dango and Weed settled in for a long, loud wait.

Chapter Eleven

It had been almost an hour, and the squealing in the back of the jail hadn't stopped.

Dango made an observation, "Ol' Jimmy Monrestic ought to be getting pretty exhausted doing all that hollering back there."

"Well dang it Dango, ain't a thing we can do for him. He wouldn't be in this predicament if he wouldn't have tried to rob us."

"From the sounds of what the sheriff said, it's a good thing he didn't just shoot us before we even knew he was there."

"You know, we really gotta get back to being keen about just letting people ride up on us. We ain't never rode that way before."

"You're dead right Weed. I suppose spending so much time lately around those we know we can trust, we've let our hunting ways get a little rusty."

"I sure hate to hear that Dango; but, I think you're right."

Ennnggg. The front door to the jail swung open, and both men stood to their feet. Expecting to see the sheriff and the doc, they were surprised when a woman who appeared to be in her early twenties stepped inside. Her complexion was similar to the color of coffee with a lot of cream. Her personality, they would find out later, was like coffee with a lot of sugar in it.

Dango's greeting was a hair faster than Weed's. "Howdy ma'am. The sheriff's gone into town. He should be getting back any time now."

Before she could reply, Weed added, "Yes ma'am. We thought that was him when you came in."

He immediately thought that sounded awkward, and tried to fix it, "I mean, we didn't think you was him. Ain't no way we'd mistake you for him."

Dango helped him out, sensing he was going down fast, "What he's trying to say ma'am is when we heard you coming in the door, we thought it was Sheriff Lee and the doc we were hearing."

The young lady was smiling ear to ear. She finally introduced herself in her deep East Texas twang. The drawl was smooth, not cutting, "Shucks gentlemen, that's alright. I'm Cassie. Cassie Canyon."

"Cassie, it's nice to meet you. I'm Dango, and this here's my good friend Weed."

Hands were being shook all around. "Weed? I never heard of anybody named Weed before."

"Nice to meet you Miss Cassie. Cassie Canyon? That's an attractive name. My name's Tumbleweed. I just go by Weed for short. It is *Miss* Cassie isn't it?"

The blush on Cassie's cheeks could be slightly seen through her coffee with cream features. "Yes sir, Mister Weed, it is *Miss* Cassie. My pa's made things a whole lot difficult when suitors came calling before."

Both men laughed. Weed finally settled his laughter and spoke up, "Well I can understand that ma'am. If I had a daughter as pretty as you, I'd make it a whole lot difficult too."

The blush on Cassie's face was getting brighter. Dango leaned over and began whispering soft lyrics in Weed's ears, soft enough that Cassie probably couldn't hear them, *"Pricilla, Pricilla."*

Dango smiled as he sang the name of Weed's bride in his ears. Weed jumped away from the singing and exclaimed, "Dango, you know better than that."

"Do I?"

"Well you darn sure ought to."

Cassie just stood there and watched, not really sure what the squabble was about, but having a real good assumption. The men noticed she was standing there silently witnessing all their verbal scuffling and they became embarrassed.

"Sorry ma'am, this isn't usually like us."

"That's fine sir. And call me Cassie."

"Oh I'm sorry ma'am, Cassie it is. And you can call me Dango."

Tumbleweed interjected, "And you can call me Weed."

"Sounds good. Where'd you say my pa went? You say he should be back soon?"

"Your pa? Who's your pa?"

Cassie turned toward Dango to reply, "The sheriff. He told me about you last time you were through here. Sorry I didn't get a chance to meet you then."

Dango did some quick reasoning work in his mind before answering back, "Ma'am…"

"Uh, uh, uh, you said you'd call me Cassie."

"Oh, that's right. Cassie, you said your name is Canyon, and you're a Miss, and your pa is the sheriff. Is all that right?"

"Yes sir."

Dango couldn't help but reply, "Uh, uh, uh, you said you'd call me Dango."

They all laughed. "That's all true Dango. I'm Cassie Canyon, Miss Cassie Canyon. And my pa is the sheriff."

Dango was working over in his mind what was riddling him like working to get a splinter out, "So you're a widow then?"

"No sir." She caught herself and corrected her statement, "I mean no Dango. Why would you think I'm a widow? I ain't never been married before."

Dango explained as Weed and Cassie looked on in anticipation, "Well, If you're a missus, and your pa is the sheriff, how come his name is Lee and yours is Canyon?"

She started giggling. "Oh, that's easy to explain. You see…"

Ennnggg. The door opened on its old hinges and stopped her replying. The three turned to see the doc and the sheriff coming in.

Sheriff Lee began as soon as he got inside, "He's right back there Doc. I'll be back there to check on things in a minute." Then he addressed the others, "I see you men have met my lovely daughter Cassie."

"As a matter of fact, we have. She was just about to tell us why her last name is Canyon and yours is Lee."

As soon as Dango said that, he had a thought that the sheriff might not be Cassie's birth dad. He was beginning to wish he wouldn't have even brought the subject up.

Sheriff Lee saved him from the discomfort, "Oh yeah, there's a funny story behind that."

Cassie took the story from there, "I'm proud to be a Lee, very honored to be the daughter of CW Lee. There was this one time though that I played the main role in a play the town put on. I was a gun toting law woman. Everybody said I was the perfect one for the part, my dad being sheriff and all."

Dango and Weed were still trying to figure out what this had to do with her last name being different from her pa's.

"I played Sheriff Canyon. It was a hoot."

Dango took a leap, "I see it now. So, you were in that play and now you want to be an actress. And that's gonna be your stage name."

"No, not at all."

Weed and Sheriff Lee both laughed.

Dango saved himself, "Okay, keep going then. I thought I had it figured out."

Cassie was still laughing as she continued, "So I was in that play. It went on every night for two weeks. They kept asking us to have it again the next night too. Finally, we just had to insist that we had to get on with our lives."

Weed took a stab at it, "So you liked the name Canyon so much, you decided to just keep it."

"Close. I liked the possibilities of being a law person, so I decided Cassie Canyon would be a fitting name for following that dream."

"So you wanna be a sheriff like your dad? I'd say he's been effective keeping his last name and sheriffing."

Cassie tried to explain, not really expecting Dango and Weed to get it. After all, it took her pa a pretty good while to get used to the notion. "I just think it's gonna be hard enough to want to do this as a woman. And no, I don't wanna be a sheriff. I want to do what y'all do."

Both men looked at her, "Huh?"

She snickered as they had both said the same thing at the same time. "I wanna chase bounties and bring them to justice. Ain't nothing scalds my hide more than someone who's done the crime and then trying to keep from paying for it."

"Wow. That's a lot to digest. I applaud you for your valiant yearnings. In all due respect, I just don't know if you know what you're asking for."

Cassie was as female as they come, pretty, feminine, curvy, tender skin, dark brown enticing eyes, moist lips; even her elbows were appealing. But she had the grit to follow through with what she endeavored. She knew that more than anybody. Just looking at her, it would appear that Dango was exactly right in his surmising. She would never be convinced otherwise though until she proved herself to be following what she was called to do in life, or let all her trying prove that she wasn't.

"I'm sorry ma'am, I didn't mean to misspeak. It's just I ain't used to such a nice-looking lady as you wanting to ride the trails hunting outlaws."

"Well, before you count me out, don't forget, I've got my daddy's blood in me."

"That's sure true Miss Cassie. That is sure true."

Chapter Twelve

"Weed, I just don't know what to think about that girl saying she wants to be a bounty hunter."

Weed was thinking about which way he wanted to go with this conversation. Before he could decide, Dango continued, "I mean, look how hard it's been on us through the years. Cotton on it, she's probably seen or heard about bad guys being brought to justice. Probably realizes the importance of bringing 'em in and putting a stop to all the hurt they're causing."

"Probably so. She likely sees all the glory of the job and not the guts."

"She doesn't even look like she has any guts at all for this kind of work."

"That's for sure. I kind'a feel like there's a whole lot more under that woman's skin than looks like though."

"Well, she is Sheriff Lee's daughter. Has to be more than just them alluring looks about her."

"Alluring? Where in the world did you pick that word up at? Alluring?"

Both men had a hearty laugh.

"Saw it in one of those dime novels."

"And I bet when you came across it, you ran and asked Pricilla what it meant."

The laughter continued.

"You're dadgummed right I did. And she told me too. She started slipping her silk scarf back and forth across the back of her neck, dancing around for me while she explained it. That helped me get a real good understanding of alluring."

"Whoa pardner. That's far enough with that. Too far actually."

Weed kept laughing at Dango's expense while Dango grew bashfully quiet.

He finally broke his silence, "Well I hope she ain't expecting us to take her on a run to help her learn the ropes."

Weed added, "I hope her pa don't want that either."

"I hadn't thought of that."

Before Weed could add more to the banter, Dango switched gears, "We gotta come up with a plan for finding ol' Clankie Claster."

"You said he was last seen escaping at Lone Creek?"

"Word I got was he got away while they were in the middle of hanging him."

"He must be some more crafty son of a gun."

"Yeah, ol' Clankie and that entire outfit he rode with were some bad hombres. Everyone of 'em deserved to hang ten times just for what I knew of 'em. And I'm sure there were things they did that I haven't even heard of."

"Maybe the sheriff will have some leads when we get back over there."

"Not likely. I'm guessing if he did, he'd lit out already and re-apprehended him. I know it wasn't him that directly let ol' Clankie get away, but I'm sure he takes it personal.

Weed interjected, "It did happen on his watch so to speak."

"Well, actually Weed, Sheriff Lee was gone fishing the week of the hanging. He didn't even know about the escape 'til he got back from his trip. From the short time I've known him, he seems to be a good man with real good abilities.

"You're sure right Dango, he's bound to be taking Clankie's get-away personal. You know things like that can even happen with good people on watch. Don't forget the time that pretty woman rode up and took that injun prisoner from you."

Dango felt almost sick at the thought. "You got a point Weed. How about let's try and forget that though."

Weed smiled. "Still won't hurt to ask the sheriff if he has any idea where he might be."

"Just as long as we don't get cornered into taking that girl of his with us."

Chapter Thirteen

Dango and Weed tied Twilight and Hay Bale out front of the jail and walked inside to find Cassie sitting at the sheriff's desk. Dango thought to himself, *I was hoping she wouldn't be here.* Weed was thinking, *Mercy she's alluring.* He pushed that thought back as quickly as possible and forced images of Pricilla into his mind.

"Howdy ma'am, uh Cassie."

"Hello Dango. Weed."

Dango got right to it, "Where's your pa? Need to go over some things with him."

"He's right back there in the back with the prisoner. I'll fetch him for you."

As she was standing up and heading that way, Sheriff Lee appeared from the back of the jail.

Dango and Weed said in harmony, "Howdy Sheriff."

"Men. Good to see y'all. I just fed Jimmy Monrestic his lunch. He should be quiet for a while."

"Good. He was being a noisy little twit last time we were here."

The sheriff smiled. "You might be too if you had bullet holes blown through both arms."

All three men grinned, thinking ol' Jimmy had asked for it and had worse than that coming to him if they could help it.

Weed mentioned, "He'll forget all about those hurt arms when he's swinging by a noose."

The sheriff noticed Cassie was taking all this in, "Cassie, grab that flyer for ol' Jimmy Monrestic out of my desk."

She reached in the sturdy, oak desk and shuffled through a few wanted posters before finding the one for Jimmy. Noticing his picture, "Yep, that's him."

She handed it to her pa. Showing it to Dango and Weed he declared, "We can take this over to the Lone Star Bank and claim your reward."

Dango and Weed both did some quick mental math when they saw the ten thousand dollar bounty poster on the outlaw. They didn't say it out loud, but each of them thought, *Five thousand dollars apiece.*

"Sounds good." Dango replied. "First though, can we talk about Clankie Claster?"

The sheriff answered, "Now that's a sticker in a sore."

"I know it is sheriff. Ain't nobody blaming you. We all know you're a fine lawman. Could've happened to any of us."

"Thanks Dango. But you know how it is. You know I won't be able to rest til he's locked back up."

"And that's just what we intend to do. You got any ideas where we might start looking around here?"

"To tell you the truth, ain't no telling. The nearest town's quite a ways from here. He could be there or anywhere between here and there. Heck, if I was him I'd be down in Mexico by now."

"Well you've certainly narrowed it down." Dango jested. Then he offered, "I suppose we'll head over to that nearest town and ask around."

Sheriff Lee advised, "Well there's a couple actually. Just ride north til you come to an old abandoned place, used to be called Farmers Crossing, just a burned down spot in the road now. Hang a right and head east. After about an hour and a half, you'll come to Trinity Creek. Not a big town, but they've got all we have here. Or turn left at the old ghost town of Farmers Crossing and go west. Ride about the same distance and you'll come to a place called Hangmans Creek."

"Ok, at least we have somewhere to start now. I don't think an outlaw would want to stop very long at a place called Hangmans Creek. May as well begin over in Trinity Creek. Sound good to you Weed?"

"Well, I think you're thinking too much like a lawman and not enough like an outlaw. If I was running from the law, I might be tempted to stay at a place with a name like that just 'cause I'd reckon the law would think just like what you just said."

"Well, we can split up and each of us take a town. Or we can both ride together and go to each place."

"This Clankie Claster has already been captured once and got away. I believe it's best if we ride in there together. For all we know, he's done met up with some more hardened gunslingers."

"Alright Weed, at least we have a plan of action. We'll hit Trinity Creek first, and on the chance that he's not there, we'll head over to Hangmans Creek. How about we stay over at Trinity Creek til morning unless we come across him before that. That'll give us some time to get a real lay of the place. Then, we can head out for the next town come sunrise.

Weed gave a nod of agreement and Dango said, "Let's ride."

Heading out the door, he added, "If it's all the same with you sheriff, we can go by the bank and collect that reward for ol' Jimmy Monrestic when we get back."

At that, they told the sheriff and Cassie bye and made it out the door without her offering to ride with them.

Little did they realize she was already forming her own plan to get to Hangmans Creek before them and scout that town out first.

Chapter Fourteen

Dango and Weed rode along at a good clip. They'd been riding like this for some time and figured to reach Trinity Creek well before sundown. They slowed their horses just long enough to approach the end of the road and make their turn.

"There's that T in the road the sheriff told us about." Weed motioned toward the end of the path.

Dango pointed to their right, noticing the abandoned town that lay desolate like it had been discarded in its prime. "Must be the ghost town he mentioned."

Weed turned to look that direction and quickly turned his head back to Dango, "Did you see that?" he exclaimed shockingly.

"See what?"

"Could've sworn I saw one of them ghosts we heard of."

Dango laughed. "Ain't called a ghost town because of ghosts Weed. It's called that because nobody is living there. Everybody who used to has disappeared or gone."

"Well I swear there was somebody moving out there."

"You're just jumpy 'cause you were expecting to see ghosts in a ghost town. Probably just a raccoon or something."

"Wouldn't hurt to check it out."

"Probably wouldn't help either. We ain't got time to be sightseeing right now. Wait til the way back. Let's stop then, when we're on the way back, after our investigating in these two other towns. What do ya say?"

"Whatever you say. But I know I saw something out there."

The two rode on, turning right and heading east at the T in the road. They were unaware that the Wild Bumpkins Gang, now comprised of Wilford Waco Waterman, Hurley Jenkins, and Clankie Claster, were at the bleak Farmers Crossing ghost town finalizing their plans for robbing the Watering Hole later that night.

They were also oblivious to the fact that Cassie Canyon would ride through here later in the evening heading to Hangmans Creek looking for the same man they were trying to find.

They could sense Twilight and Hay Bale were feeling good, so they hit it hard and reached Trinity Creek in just over an hour after making the turn at Farmers Crossing. Riding over a manmade board bridge, they sensed this passage probably got covered during the rainy season. Palmetto plants were abundant, and the surrounding ground area looked dark like it never became fully dry. Dango and Weed took this as a sign that the place probably flooded often.

Today, the creek was down enough and they traveled over the wooden bridge easily, their horse's hooves clomping. It was early evening, and the setting sun was allowing a comfortable coolness to settle into the air. A constant breeze seemed to be pushing the sun gently away and pulling a nippiness in for the evening. The humid air would help the chilliness be felt to the bone.

"Ain't never been here before."

"Can't say that I have either Weed. I was just down this way not long ago, and I didn't even know this town was over here."

"How about we get a bite and wet our whistle before looking around."

"Sounds like a plan. Actually, we'll be taking care of several orders of business by doing that. We can fill our bellies, quench our thirst, and talk to some of the locals at the same time. Maybe ask around and see if anyone's heard anything about ol' Clankie."

"Seems like everything here in Trinity Creek is all right there together, doesn't it?"

Weed looked around and took in what Dango was referring to. It appeared at first glance that all of the town's businesses were in fairly close proximity to each other. Painted handwriting was scrawled across fronts of buildings to indicate what kind of commerce took place inside each one.

Dango and Weed saw the business names of Tony's Tastes and Tap, Ben Miser's Mortuary, the Trinity Creek Livery and Stables, Doc Gillon's practice, and the Indian Hen Trading Post. There was also a blacksmith operation without a formal name, a barber shop with the words Barney's Barbering and Tailoring on the sign, and another structure with the word JAIL painted out front.

Dango said, "I wonder if that Ben Miser is kin to ol' Fred Miser the mortician up in Timber Creek, Colorado?"

"That's a long way from here. Could be though. Sure a heck of a coincidence if he ain't." Weed pointed to another sign, this one was pretty well made, "And what about that'un? Doc Gillon. Reckon he's kin to the doc over in Lone Creek? Or you figure maybe it's the same doc. You think he does the doctoring in both cities?"

"Sure possible. It's quite a ways over here from Lone Creek though. I'd wager he's a cousin or brother or something. And how about that Tony's Tastes and Tap? I reckon a feller can get a meal and a drink in there."

"Makes sense. Let's get Twilight and Hay Bale over to the Trinity Creek Livery and head to Tony's and find out how hot the meals are and how cool the drinks are."

"You read my mind."

Chapter Fifteen

"Now Waco, remember, when we get there, I'm the one who starts it by saying loudly *This is a holdup! Everybody get your hands up*! You and Hurley have your guns drawn, aiming them at everybody in the place. Be sure you don't miss anybody. Gotta get a good dose of fear in 'em. Make 'em know we're in charge. I'll grab the cash from the day's take. We'll be out of there quicker than you can say We're the Wild Bumpkins Gang."

Wilford and Hurley grinned big enough that their missing and yellow tinted teeth were obvious.

Wilford suggested, "We don't need to be in thare too long. The sheriff's liable to show up if'n we are."

"Clankie yakked at him, "Don't matter if he does Wilford! You're thinking like a scared man. We ain't the ones who's afraid! We're the ones bringing the fear! *We* make *them* afraid! If that sheriff shows up, we'll just put a plug in him! You wanna be a Waco or a Wilford?"

Wilford tried to suggest another notion to prove he was a Waco, "Hows about when we go in, I go to the bar and order a firewater. Then we catch 'em by surprise and get the drop on 'em?"

"Ain't necessary. We'll just storm in there, guns raised, and take 'em for all they've got. Won't be a hornswabbling thing they can do about it. Not one blasted thing!"

Wilford and Hurley just looked at each other like they knew Clankie had all the answers. After all, he used to ride with the Zulu Outlaws.

"I sure would like a firewater tho."

"Wilford, don't be a horndog. You can get all the firewater you want after we're done taking 'em for all they're worth. Gotta be a ton of dough in that place after a full day's take."

Wilford felt deflated, felt like he hadn't lived up to Clankie's expectations for a Waco. But he was happy about the firewater part. "Sounds like a good way to go about it Mr. Clankie."

"Don't you ever call me mister! I ain't no flipping superior uppity! I'm a decent hard working human being! You can call me Clankie or Claster, or Clankie Claster! Heck, you can even call me boss if you want to as long as it's realized you mean the boss of an outlaw gang. But you best not ever call me mister again! You do, and it'll be the last time you ever say anything to anybody!"

Wilford literally shook in his boots, not saying a thing for a few long minutes, "You got it boss. Far as I see it, from now on you're the boss of the Wild Bumpkins Gang."

"Works for me too." Hurley said weakly but definitely.

"Fine. We got that settled. Get them firearms ready for robbing. Make sure they're loaded and you've got plenty extra ammo. We'll head out soon."

Dango and Weed had spent at least a couple of hours getting their horses taken care of and moseying over to Tony's Taste and Tap for the best grub they'd had since leaving Lone Creek. So far, most of those they asked had given no useful information concerning Clankie Claster. A handful said they thought they might've seen a man in town that could be the desperado.

Everybody had heard rumors and wild stories about the escape, but few would fess up to having maybe seen hide or hair of the desperado.

"Reckon they're just too scared to say anything Dango?"

"Could be. But usually there's at least one who's too brave or too stupid to be scared. Seems like it might be a dry hole so far."

"Yeah, at least we had a good meal. Might be though that the few who say they may have seen him could be on to something."

Dango's body language agreed whole heartedly to that. "How about we ask around town some more just to be sure." He said this more as a statement instead of a question.

Weed nodded, "Maybe we should stick around til morning and then go on over to Hangmans Creek."

At this, they got up at once to head out of Tony's.

A deep mist had set in, covering the ground with a steamy haze. The three installed members of the Wild Bumpkins Gang rode along determined. The hooves of their horse's feet bounced up and down, in and out of the low-settled fog.

No wind was blowing at all, and the fog floated firm against the ground. The thick, gray, low-lying precipitation could be seen a little in the dark by the riders thanks to the illumination of the bright, full moon that hung low overhead.

The stern face of Clankie helped his words have meaning to Hurley and Wilford. "Don't forget, charge in there with your guns raised, and demand everybody to get their hands up. Say it as mean as you can. Don't let anybody have any doubts about what's going on in there when we show up. They gotta all know we're there to rob the place. Got that?"

Before they could answer, Clankie continued ranting, "Check your guns. Make sure you got 'em loaded. And don't accidentally shoot each other."

At this, they both started laughing.

"Ain't nothing to laugh about! I've seen it happen before. Either of you by chance shoot me, you best hope it ends me. Otherwise, I'll kill you along with anybody else I choose to in there."

Hurley and Wilford each got a resolute look on his face, trying to look grim to prove to Clankie they didn't have it in them to unintentionally shoot each other or him. He didn't believe their looks and thought they were both quite capable of doing just that. "I'll be sure to watch out for y'all's cross-fire. Don't dillydally about shooting anybody that needs it. Just watch your aim is all."

It was a couple hours before midnight, and the place was winding down. Customers knew they better drink fast. The workers knew they were about to get to go home for the night.

Wilford wanted to just go in casually, order a drink, chug it down, and then spill the beans that they were there for the valuables. Hurley would be good with that plan too, but they both knew who was running the show. And Clankie had pulled no punches when letting them know how this would go down. This was his modus operandi, his mode of operating. Generally, Clankie liked to go in guns a blazing. He had found this method to be tried and true, having stormed in many a place and seen a lot of men and even women killed at his hands while he left untouched, unhurt.

Pulling up just in front of the place, they dismounted quickly and headed inside the Watering Hole. Clankie didn't have to put on his game face; he wore a permanent evil look about him. He instructed the other two, "Put your monster faces on."

They didn't have to ask what he meant, and they both purposefully formed the meanest scowls they could manage on their faces and lifted their guns in front of them while hurrying in the front door of the place.

Chapter Sixteen

Dango and Weed figured they'd head over to see the sheriff of Trinity Creek as soon as they finished with their meal. This settlement was different from Lone Creek in that everything was closer together. They didn't have to ride out of town and go a ways to get to the jail. It was just up the road a bit.

They didn't even bother collecting the horses yet. Enjoying the walk and taking in all the sights of the place, their minds were determined, realizing a killer was somewhere on the loose. Determination was rising, as each of them was ready to find the fugitive and bring him to justice. The image of Clankie Claster was at the forefront of their thinking. Everywhere they looked, they were diligent to keep their eyes out for him. Their vigilance was heightened.

"It'll sure be nice if the sheriff can tell us where to find that desperado."

"Yep, but how likely is it? Same as I said about Sheriff Lee over in Lone Creek; if he knows, don't you think he would already have tried to go get him?"

"You're probably right."

"I'm just as ready to catch that maniac as you are Weed. For one thing, he needs to be locked away where he can't hurt anybody else. For another thing, I've been missing Savanna something fierce."

Weed laughed. They had ridden trails in all kinds of weather; rain, sunshine, thunderstorms, hailstorms, blizzards. They had chased outlaws who had killed their own kin. They had arrested some bounties during the daytime and others late at night. Neither of them had ever given the impression of wanting to be anywhere else except right where they were at the time. Things seemed different now than they ever had.

"I know what you mean Dango? You reckon we're getting old? Being around that girl Cassie has got me to noticing how bad I miss Pricilla."

"No Weed, I don't think it's just being older. I think we both have ladies now in our lives who mean more to us than any woman ever has."

Weed forced himself to give a big chuckle, "Look at us getting all mushy."

"Yeah, look at us. They'll still be there when we get back. We got a devil posing as a man to catch up with."

The laughter stopped, and each man's face grew a grim look on it. Their laughing as well as the grimness of their looks were both coping strategies they had unconsciously adopted to help maintain while away from the two best things that had ever happened to either of them. They didn't know that Savanna and Pricilla were fighting the same struggles, wishing their men would hurry home.

It wasn't very long of a walk until they reached the jail. Walking inside, the first person they saw was the sheriff.

"Hello gentleman. Sheriff Reevers."

It didn't take long for all three men to shake hands and pass names around. Dango filled the sheriff in on their hunt for Clankie Claster. In a few words, the sheriff informed them that he didn't have a clue about the escapee, wished he did, but wishes wouldn't get them any closer to finding him.

Sheriff Reevers was a young man of thirty something. He looked like he would make it easy in any occupation that required a man with dark hair, good looks, and charm. He had the gift of gab, and it wasn't long before Dango and Weed knew he'd never married, his pa had been sheriff of another town, and his granpappy had been warden at a prison farm not too far from Trinity Creek.

"I'll tell you what chaps, after y'all find that Clankie Claster, come on back; I've got a few bandits I'd like to send you after. They've been on the run so long, the pay will probably be double that of anything else you'll find."

They listened to him talk for a while longer and finally made their exit. Dango and Weed had encountered several folks over the years with the same gift for talking as Sheriff Reevers. Neither of them had ever figured out a way to make a clean exit. They usually just ended up waiting and waiting until the talker finally ran out of air and ended the discourse himself or herself.

"Dango took a jab at it when Sheriff Reevers drew a quick breath, and it actually worked this time, "Weed, how about we go ahead and head over to Hangmans Creek. You never know, we just might get lucky."

Weed was nodding in agreement as Sheriff Reevers opened his mouth again, "Speaking of getting lucky…"

They shook hands hastily while he was in mid-sentence and headed hurriedly out the door like they knew where the outlaw was and had to get over there quickly before he left.

Sheriff Reevers stopped in the middle of what he was saying and exclaimed, "Y'all be sure and come back after you catch him. I've got plenty to keep you busy."

Both bounty hunters shook their heads as if in agreement, knowing Colorado was already calling them to come back.

Chapter Seventeen

As the trio of bandit outlaws rushed into the Watering Hole, their guns were being raised. They all stormed the same direction, making a bee line to the center of the rear of the large front room of the place. This brought them directly in front of the bar as patrons were becoming wide-eyed, noticing what was abruptly happening.

Intoxicated customers filled the place. Strong whisky and warm beer had been poured for hours. Before any of the Wild Bumpkins Gang said a word, drunks started jumping down to the floor. There was actually more falling being done than jumping as they staggered to get out of the way of bullets that might get fired from the robber's already brandished pistols.

Clankie was forming the words and just about to let them fly out of his mouth when a deafening blast made a booming noise. A full bottle of rotgut whisky exploded behind the bar from a bullet accidentally fired from Wilford's gun.

Clankie immediately looked at him like he was definitely no Waco. The stare didn't last long, and he went back to business as usual. "This is a hold up! Everybody get your hands where we can see 'em!"

The Watering Hole owner, who had been behind the bar serving drinks to drunks raised his hands as high as he could get them right away. Thankful the wild, stray bullet from the outlaw's gun hadn't hit him, he intended to do as ordered with zero amount of hesitation.

Just as he complied, Clankie aimed from about eight feet away and dropped the man lifeless with one deadly squeeze of the trigger of his Volcanic pistol.

Next, Clankie headed straight for the till and began pulling out greenbacks. Emptying the cashbox, he screamed, "Where's the safe in this place? There's got to be more than this!"

When nobody answered his ranting demands, he pointed his heavy pistol at the crowd on the floor. "Somebody better tell me what I want, or I'll start shooting every blasted one of you."

Hurley Jenkins decided to get in the fight, "He'll do it too. I done seen him kill a bank full of people in less than thirty seconds."

Hurley, Wilford, and Clankie all knew this was a lie, but somehow each of the outlaws had quick, narcissistic daydreams that helped them to believe it to be true.

Nobody moved or said a word. Clankie started firing, and five regulars went from being sloppy drunk to messy dead as quick as boom, boom, boom, boom, boom!

The ones on the floor who were still alive hunkered more, fearing they would be next. Clankie fumed down a hallway looking for the safe he knew had to be here somewhere. Hurley and Wilford both followed behind him. As soon as Clankie noticed this, he turned to them,

"You old galoots, somebody's gotta watch them people laying on the floor in there."

Hurley and Wilford jarred into each other as they bumped back down the hall passage to go watch the victims. Aiming their guns at the people on the floor gave each of them a sense of power. After a few minutes, Clankie could be heard yelling from the back of the place, "Here it is! I found it!"

A few minutes more, and he came running back up the hall with a bag filled to the brim with stolen greenbacks. Hurley and Wilford headed for the door, thinking they were ready to rush out and head to the gang's hideout.

"Where are y'all going? You just gonna let all the treasures these folks are holding be left behind?"

Neither of them were sure of what Clankie was referring to until he started reaching down himself and taking things from those who were lying on the floor. All three men went to grabbing stuff from scared customers, the dead ones and the live ones, and after a while, they were satisfied that they had it all.

As Clankie finally headed to the front door of the place to make his getaway, Hurley and Wilford took the cue and followed him out, trying to act as though they'd done this a thousand times.

All three men felt fulfilled, knowing they'd done what they came to do. Each one was looking shortly into the future, anticipating being back at Farmers Crossing, counting and splitting up the take they'd gotten from the Watering Hole. As they made their exit, none of the three outlaws noticed the coffee with cream complected woman who had just ridden up in the dark outside the Watering Hole.

The gang charged off in the darkness, low lingering fog hovering just above the ground, the moon shining enough to light the way for the riders. Heading toward Farmers Crossing were Clankie Claster, Hurley Jenkins, the self-acclaimed Waco Waterman, and the woman they didn't see or hear following them, Cassie Canyon.

Chapter Eighteen

"Those drunks at the Watering Hole probably won't even remember being killed in the morning."

Wilford and Hurley laughed at what Clankie had just said even though they didn't really understand it. They were both straining to figure out how the ones Clankie killed would remember it in the morning. Still they laughed.

Reaching Farmers Crossing, each man dismounted and headed into the run down dwelling that had more to it than any of the other structures around. Most of the buildings had been burned to the ground or just plain deteriorated from years of not being used.

Clankie held tightly to the money bag. Wilford and Hurley followed close behind. Just as they went to enter the rundown shack of a partially standing building, something caught Clankie's eye. Looking intently in the direction of the movement, he peered into the blackness of night.

Not seeing anything, he jerked his well-used revolver from its holster and fired two quick shots in that direction. When he did, somebody or something started scrambling as if trying to get out of the way of the bullets.

Before Hurley and Wilford could decide how to react to Clankie's actions, shots came at them from the area the scrambling had just taken place at.

"Scram!" Cassie shooed her horse with a hush of a scream to make him run off and get him out of danger. Then she jumped behind what was left of an old horse buggy. She fired again, aiming at the three silhouettes about forty feet from her.

The three shapes she was firing at all dove to find cover and began shooting back. Clankie was a hardened veteran of such goings on, and he meant to kill whoever was trying to ambush them. Wilford and Hurley hadn't ever really been in something this exciting, though they'd lied frequently of times just like this that they had been part of.

Clankie tried his best to whisper and make hand motions in the dimness of the shadowy surroundings to the old codgers, trying to get them to help him flank whoever was attacking them. He was growing more and more frustrated while struggling to get them to circle around and close the shooter in.

Finally, his endeavors paid off, and they seemed to understand what he wanted. Hurley and Wilford would swear later, if they made it out of this alive, that they had dodged whizzing bullets as they hummed by their heads.

The men charged in a wide circular path, creating a perimeter around the assailant. By the time Cassie recognized what they were attempting to do, it seemed too late to think of a plan to prevent it from happening.

Why in the world did I allow myself to get in such a predicament? Her thoughts chastised her for letting such odds come up against her. It was her own fault. She should have thought it out ahead of time and not permitted herself to get cornered in by these deadly outlaws.

As they began closing in the circle around her, she continued firing, hoping to inflict enough danger or harm to stop their assault. However, their bullets were spraying all around her, and she hoped and prayed that at any moment she wouldn't be killed here tonight.

Just then, she realized she was firing one bullet for each of their three. Hopelessness and helplessness covered her hard. She'd never felt so doomed as right here, right now.

They were closing in, near enough for her to hear the wild screams of the mad men. The sounds of bullets leaving the guns and the sounds of the bullets hitting the ground all around her were deafening. She found a resolve within her and kept shooting back, determined not to die without putting up a fierce fight.

Boom! Boom! Boom! Boom! Boom! Boom! Boom! Boom! A new barrage of shots came from the dark.

"What in tarnation is that?" Clankie Claster shrieked in shock as shots began being fired from outside the circle he and the other members of the Wild Bumpkins Gang had formed around their attacker. The three men didn't know whether to keep tightening the circle around who they now knew was one lone person or turn the fight on whoever was now shooting at them from behind.

"You two, keep shooting at our attacker! I'll head off whoever's firing those new shots!" Clankie gave his orders and headed toward the location of the latest volley of shots. Wilford and Hurley continued shooting in the direction they thought they were supposed to shoot.

Cassie noticed the firefight was taking a sudden turn in her favor. Unexpectedly, she was able to leave her hiding place and rush the area where the shots were being fired from. They seemed to be uncontrolled shots now, being fired wide right and left.

She dashed upon the site she knew the shooters were at and discovered two old-timers firing excitedly. It seemed their eyes were clenched tightly as they pulled the triggers of their guns. Realizing she didn't even need to fire another shot at the two, she demanded in a high-pitched confident voice, "You two throw them guns down!"

Hurley and Wilford were caught by surprise and didn't hesitate to do as instructed. In short time, Cassie grabbed their guns and had them both shackled.

"You two stay here." She knew they weren't going anywhere, said it more to entertain her own self really.

Then she headed toward the sounds of the all-out shooting brawl that was still going on between whoever else was still out there fighting.

As she drew nearer, she could see one mean looking hombre behind cover firing into the shadows. After staying concealed for a few minutes, she caught a glimpse at the ones the mean hombre was firing at. *Well lookie there.* She thought to herself with comfort and relief. Peeking from cover and firing at the mean looking man were the two she would've selected to be here if she had her choice.

Instead of yelling for Dango and Weed to let them know she was okay, she lifted her rifle and fired once, hitting Clankie Claster in the gut. The fight seeped out of him rapidly. He fell in pain, dropping his gun and instinctively pulling himself into a fetal position.

After she was sure her shot had hit its mark, she yelled, "Dango! Weed! I'm over here! He's been hit!"

The bounty hunters cautiously left their hiding spots and slipped towards Cassie. When they were reunited, she showed them where Clankie Claster was lying injured with a gut-shot. After they secured him, she led them to the two old men she had shackled.

Cassie mentioned, "I sure am glad y'all showed up. They had me cornered, and I would've probably been dead in another minute or so."

Dango asserted, "Cotton on it Cassie, if it wasn't for you, we would still be fighting. You did a heck of a job out here today."

Weed nodded his head in agreement. The three went to work getting the bad guys mounted on horses for the long ride to Lone Creek.

"Maybe he won't bleed out before we get back to town."

Cassie and Weed heard Dango's words, but neither offered words of hope that the outlaw would last until they got back to Lone Creek to the doc.

The fog had risen, and the procession of horses and riders went on through the darkness, riding through the haze that seemed to envelop them as they rode.

Weed broke the silenceas they trotted along, "It'll be the wee hours of the night when we get to Doc Gillons office. You think we oughta wake him that time of night?"

Dango replied, "Let's decide when we get there."

Chapter Nineteen

As much as the three law enforcers wanted to let the doc sleep till daylight, they went ahead and woke him when they got to Lone Creek. They decided to keep watch on Clankie, Wilford, and Hurley till morning and then notify Sheriff Lee.

They went ahead and just kept all three prisoners at Doc Gillon's office, still shackled. It was a long morning as Dango, Weed, and Cassie each insisted to stay and keep watch on the three apprehended fugitives.

Clankie had lost a ton of blood, probably wouldn't have made it till morning if they hadn't made the decision to rouse the doctor. Even with all the blood he had lost, he was still continuing to curse the three apprehenders for all he was worth. They'd tell you that wasn't much though.

Wilford and Hurley didn't have any trouble sleeping. It was as though neither had a real clue as to the trouble they were facing. Somehow, in their consciousness, they felt like heroes, like they had accomplished something larger than life.

Doc had operated on Clankie and bandaged him as best as possible. The evil man had been spouting curses when he fell into a sullen, ether induced lull Doc Gillon had triggered with his general anesthesia.

As soon as Clankie was conscious enough, after the operation, he was swearing more from the extreme pain that was mixed with his typical chronic sourness. Doc had dug the lead out of his gut. The dose of ether did little to give Clankie relief from the pain of the bullet wound and the cutting Doc had done on him. Doc had an ethical battle of giving Clankie enough ether to keep him quiet and asleep, or to give him less and cause him more suffering.

"Here, let me give you a little more medicine. This will help you rest."

Clankie spurted his normal language replying to the doc's compassionate offer, "You just hurry up and give it to me. Ain't no sense in me having to lay here hurting like this. You just wait till I'm better. I'll end up killing you and them three that brought me in."

Doc tried his best to ignore the man, trying his best to see him as a patient and not as the vicious criminal he knew him to be. The struggle was hard. Doc did as best as he could and watched the man fall deeper into slumber very soon after the drugs were administered.

Just at sunrise, Weed and Cassie loaded Wilford Waterman and Hurley Jenkins and carted them over to the jail. Sheriff Lee was stirring already and was genuinely surprised when they shuffled in with the two old handcuffed men.

"Sheriff, these two were caught holding up the Watering Hole over in Hangmans Creek with Clankie Claster."

The sheriff looked at Weed as he responded to what he had just told him, "Ol' Clankie got away again?"

Weed immediately answered the sheriff's question, "No sir, he's over at Doc's place. Doc had to get a bullet out of him put there by dear Cassie. Dango's over there keeping watch."

The sheriff repositioned his stare from looking at Weed to eyeing Cassie. "That so Cassie? How'd that come about?"

His query wasn't a *how dare you* question. Rather, it was a sincere attempt to learn how his precious daughter ended up in the same proximity with such a murderer as Clankie Claster and ended up firing the shot that helped lead to his capture.

Before he got the answers he wanted, Wilford and Hurley were placed in lock up where they promptly fell back to sleep. Then, Weed and Cassie filled Sheriff Lee in on the happenings at the Wild Bumpkins Gang's hideout at Farmers Crossings.

He was worried, grateful, and proud all at the same time. Worried at thinking of what could have happened out there during that shootout with the determined escapees. Grateful that Cassie was okay. Proud that she proved to herself and them that she was indeed capable of fulfilling her dream of taking bad guys into custody.

Albeit, she would be the first to insist that things would have been a whole lot different if Dango and Weed had not been there. Of course, Dango and Weed would say the same thing about things being different if Cassie would not have been there.

Chapter Twenty

A week had gone by, and a lot had happened in that week. Clankie had recovered enough to stand trial for the many atrocities he had committed. These included the escape from the hangman's noose, the holdup at the Watering Hole, and the senseless murdering of those he killed during that robbery.

He had been easily found guilty and sentenced to be hung by the neck until dead. His accomplices, Wilford Waco Waterman and Hurley Jenkins were each sentenced to twenty years at the Westham prison farm. As old as they were, it might as well have been a death sentence. They would spend the remainder of their days at Westham telling tales of the time they spent running with the notorious Clankie Claster.

Dango and Weed were unwavering in their determination to stick around Texas long enough to see Clankie Claster hang. They were both homesick and missed Savannah and Pricilla immensely. However, they were resolute to not head back to Colorado until they watched Clankie hang. They would see it with their own eyes; then they could be satisfied heading back home, knowing the embodiment of evil that existed in that man would never be free to kill again.

While they waited for the date with the executioner, they rode over to see Sheriff Reevers in Trinity Creek and let him know they would be heading back home soon. Cassie Canyon rode along with them, as they'd formed a tight bond through their endeavors of capturing the Wild Bumpkins Gang together.

After an enjoyable ride, the three arrived at Trinity Creek and headed straight to the jail. When they walked inside, the sheriff was sitting at his desk sorting several wanted posters. He stood up at once and greeted them.

As hands were shaking, Dango and Weed noticed instantly that Sheriff Reevers was not paying any attention to them. While he was shaking their hands, his eyes were on the coffee with cream complected woman.

"Sheriff, this is Cassie Canyon. Sheriff Lee's daughter from over in Lone Creek." Dango introduced.

"Yes, yes, I've heard of Sheriff Lee in Lone Creek. Didn't know he had such an attractive daughter."

Cassie blushed as she allowed him to take her hand and kiss the back of it gently.

Dango and Weed tried their best to let Sheriff Reevers know they appreciated his earlier offer of bounty work, but they were heading back to Colorado soon. They didn't feel like he really heard all that they were saying, as all his attention was focused on Cassie.

The attraction was immediate and intense between the two. Dango and Weed didn't know who said it first, but they knew Sheriff Reevers and Cassie Canyon had each said more than once, "Just think, you were right down the road all this time, and I didn't even know you."

From that day forward, they would not let the sun go down without seeing each other every day, whether they were together the entire day or just a portion of the day. Cassie would satisfy her drive to catch bandits over the next six months, going after some of Sheriff Reever's bounties. After that, her passion for that would wane and Sheriff Reever's proposal would take the front seat. They would marry, and her bounty chasing days would give way to child rearing.

Before all of that happened though, Cassie, Dango, and Weed would head back to Lone Creek together and claim the huge reward for Clankie Claster. They would split the money three ways. Dango and Weed added that to the money they'd received for bringing in Jimmy Monrestic.

The day Clankie was hung, a sense of sadness came over Dango and Weed. The bluesy feeling came as a result of realizing people like him existed at all. They were homesick and would be oh so glad to see Savannah and Pricilla; but, as long as people like Clankie Claster were on the prowl, they would never truly lose the thrill and need for the hunt completely.

The End